MOKI and the BEES

WRITTEN BY
Helen Thorne

ILLUSTRATED BY
Debra Thorne

First published in
Great Britain in 2023 by
THORNE & THORNE
ISBN 978-1-3999-5735-9

Text copyright © 2023
Helen Thorne

Illustrations copyright © 2023
Debra Thorne

Moki loved honey.

She put it on her porridge.

She put it on her toast.

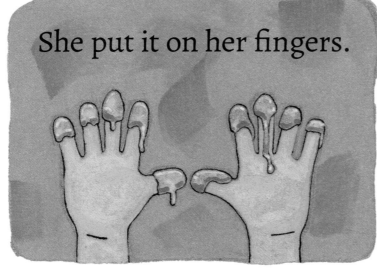

She put it on her fingers.

She even put it on the cat!

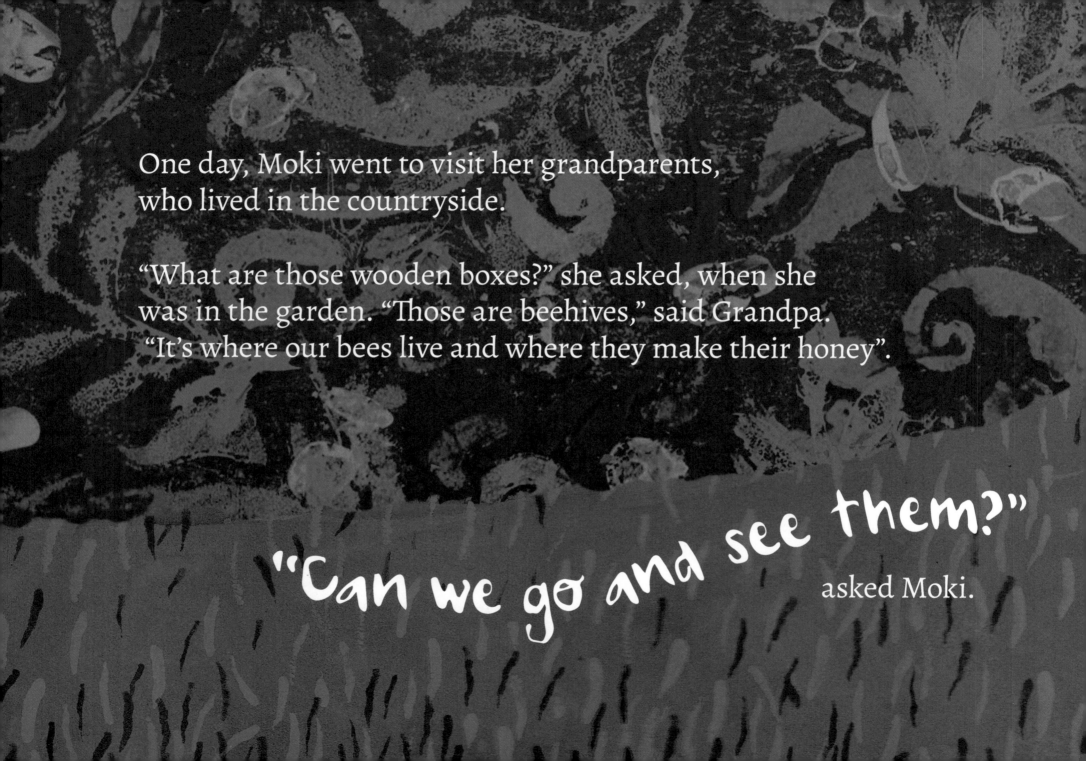

One day, Moki went to visit her grandparents,
who lived in the countryside.

"What are those wooden boxes?" she asked, when she
was in the garden. "Those are beehives," said Grandpa.
"It's where our bees live and where they make their honey".

"Can we go and see them?"
asked Moki.

"Definitely,"
said Grandpa.

Gran and Grandpa put on their bee suits.
There was one for Moki too. And gloves.

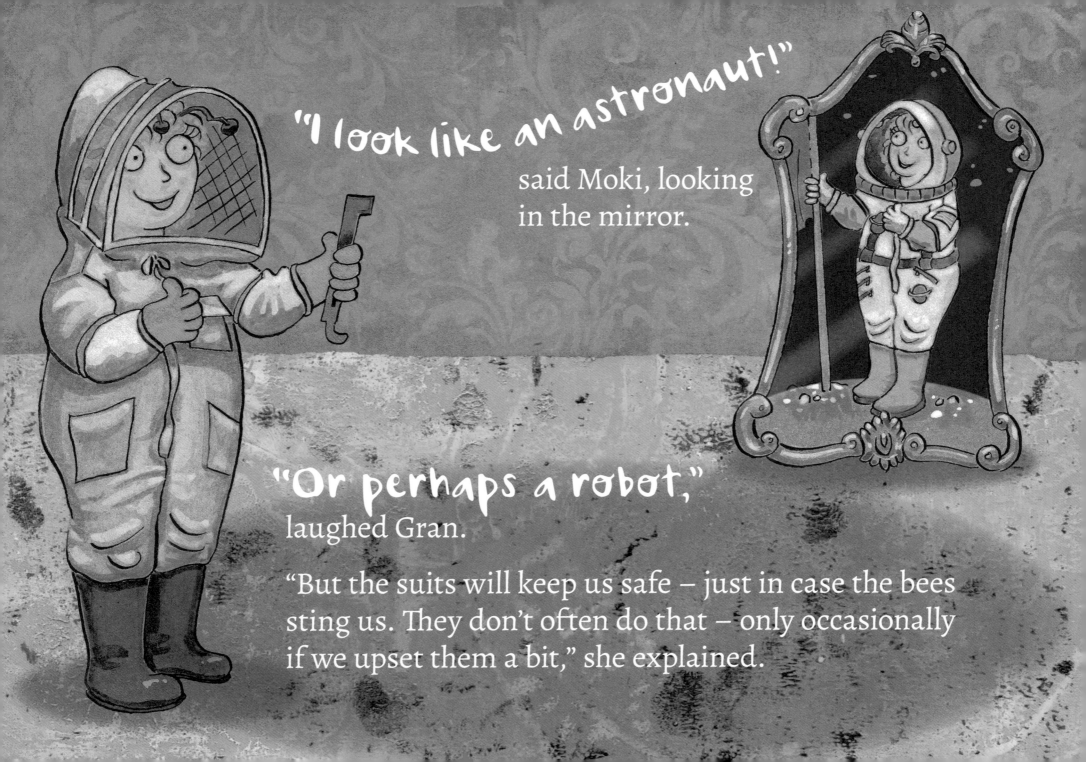

"I look like an astronaut!"

said Moki, looking in the mirror.

"Or perhaps a robot,"

laughed Gran.

"But the suits will keep us safe – just in case the bees sting us. They don't often do that – only occasionally if we upset them a bit," she explained.

"What's that?"

asked Moki, looking at an old
metal can with some leather
and a handle on it.

"It's a smoker,"

said Gran.

"We light a little fire inside it, and
the smoke calms the bees down.
That can be your job Moki."

Gran quietly lifted the roof off the hive.

They puffed some smoke in. She could hear the gentle hum of the bees.

"There are about thirty thousand bees in here Moki," said Gran.
"Just imagine that!"

"We need to find the queen bee today Moki," said Grandpa,
"to check that she's alive and laying lots of eggs."

"But how can we find her in all these bees?"
asked Moki, watching the bees.

"It's easy when you know how," said Grandpa.

And there she was.

She was a bit bigger than the other bees –
but more slender too and a lighter colour.

"She's lovely," said Moki – "and all the other bees are looking after her!"

And they were. Moki could see the worker bees feeding the queen. They were even stroking her.

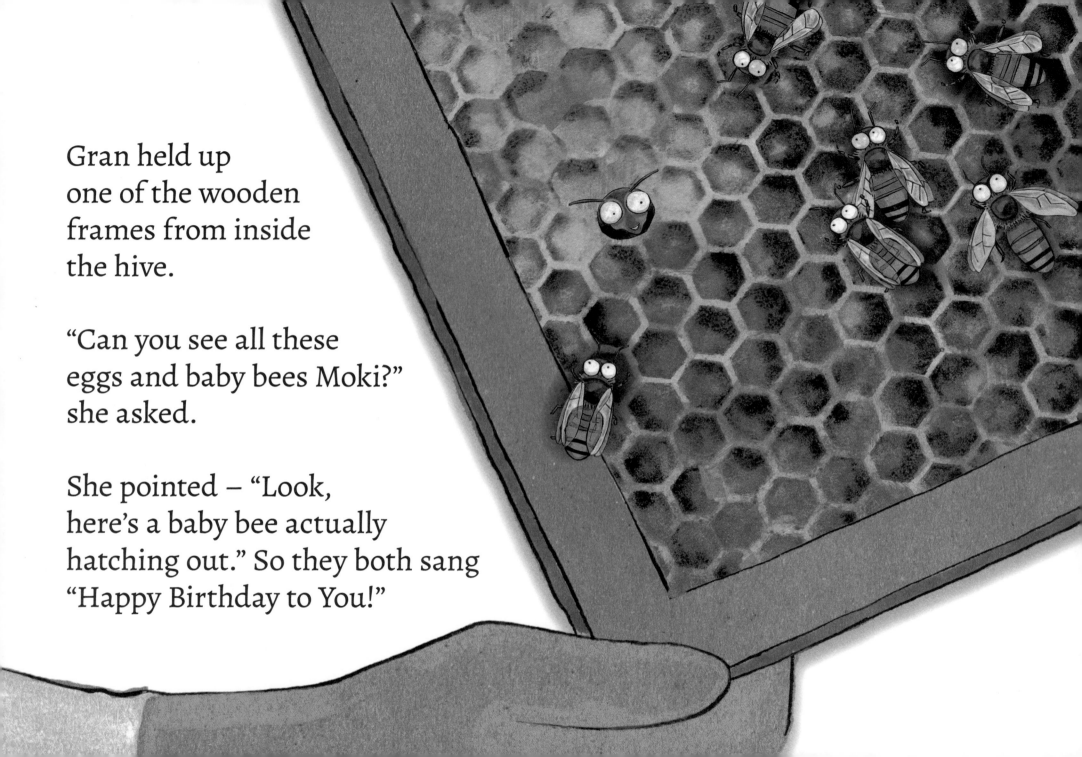

Gran held up
one of the wooden
frames from inside
the hive.

"Can you see all these
eggs and baby bees Moki?"
she asked.

She pointed – "Look,
here's a baby bee actually
hatching out." So they both sang
"Happy Birthday to You!"

"Who's that big bee there?"

asked Moki.

"Well spotted," said Grandpa. "He's a drone.
The workers are all female and the drones are the male bees."

"Shall we collect some honey now?" asked Gran.

Moki nodded and smoked the bees again.

"We should never be greedy and take too much honey," said Gran.

"We must always remember that the bees need honey for food to survive the winter, so that they can pollinate the flowers in summer."

Gran gently shook the bees off the wooden frames, and put them into a box.
"Let's take them indoors Moki."

"Now the sticky fun starts!"

Indoors, Grandpa cut the wax capping off the top of the wooden frames.

Moki could see the honey oozing out.
Grandpa put the frames full of honey into
a big, round metal container.

He showed Moki how to turn the handle
fast, to spin the honey off the frames.

Moki did it.

"Look Moki," said Gran,

"Here comes your honey."

And Moki watched as the golden honey poured out of the bottom of the spinner.

"I did it!"

said Moki.

"Well, you and the bees did it," smiled Grandpa.

Together, they poured the honey into jars and stuck labels on to them.

Moki laughed.

"Thank you bees,"

she said, as Gran gave her a jar to take home.

And Moki put her honey...

...on her porridge.

She put it on her toast.

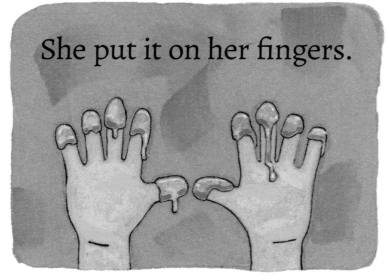

She put it on her fingers.

But...

... this time, she didn't put any on the cat.

Because that would be a waste.

Wouldn't it...?